ABOUT THE BANK STREET READY-TO-READ SERIES

More than seventy-five years of educational research, innovative teaching, and quality publishing have earned The Bank Street College of Education its reputation as America's most trusted name in early childhood education.

Because no two children are exactly alike in their development, the Bank Street Ready-to-Read series is written on three levels to accommodate the individual stages of reading readiness of children ages three through eight.

○ *Level 1:* GETTING READY TO READ **(Pre-K–Grade 1)**
Level 1 books are perfect for reading aloud with children who are getting ready to read or just starting to read words or phrases. These books feature large type, repetition, and simple sentences.

○ *Level 2:* READING TOGETHER **(Grades 1–3)**
These books have slightly smaller type and longer sentences. They are ideal for children beginning to read by themselves who may need help.

○ *Level 3:* I CAN READ IT MYSELF **(Grades 2–3)**
These stories are just right for children who can read independently. They offer more complex and challenging stories and sentences.

All three levels of the Bank Street Ready-to-Read books make it easy to select the books most appropriate for your child's development and enable him or her to grow with the series step by step. The levels purposely overlap to reinforce skills and further encourage reading.

We feel that making reading fun is the single most important thing anyone can do to help children become good readers. We hope you will become part of Bank Street's long tradition of learning through sharing.

The Bank Street College of Education

For Molly Davies, the last in her
class to lose a tooth, and
Karah and Blaire Preiss, who believe in a
recycling tooth fairy.
—B.H.H.

Special thanks
to Sandi Mendelson

THE MYSTERY OF THE MISSING TOOTH

A Bantam Book/March 1997

Published by Bantam Doubleday Dell Books
for Young Readers, a division of Bantam
Doubleday Dell Publishing Group, Inc.
1540 Broadway, New York, New York 10036.

Series graphic design by Alex Jay/Studio J

Special thanks to Jane Feder and Kathy Huck.

ISBN: 0-553-37580-6

Published simultaneously in the United States and Canada
PRINTED IN THE UNITED STATES OF AMERICA
0 9 8 7 6 5 4 3 2 1

The Mystery of the Missing Tooth

by William H. Hooks
Illustrated by Nancy Poydar

A Byron Preiss Book

BANTAM BOOKS
NEW YORK • TORONTO • LONDON • SYDNEY • AUCKLAND

Sue lost a tooth.
Jim lost a tooth.
Ben and Bill each lost a tooth
on the very same day.

Everyone in Kara's class
lost a tooth.
Everyone except Kara.

They all had cool gaps
in their teeth
when they smiled.

Everyone except Kara.
She did not smile
in class anymore.

In show-and-tell,
everyone told about the gifts
they got from the Tooth Fairy:

"I got a book,"
said Sue.

"I got money,"
said Jim.

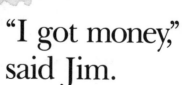

"I got color markers," said Tanya.

Kara wished she had a story about the Tooth Fairy.

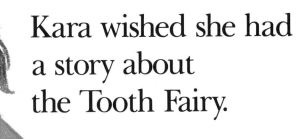

Kara told a story about Jon,
her baby brother.
"He has no teeth at all," she said.

She checked her teeth.

Nothing wiggled.
"Maybe the
Tooth Fairy
forgot me,"
said Kara.

The next morning,
Kara brushed her teeth.
Her front tooth wiggled!

Kara wiggled her tooth
on the bus to school . . .

all day long . . .

and all the way home.

13

That night she dreamed
about the Tooth Fairy.

The next day
Kara's tooth was very wiggly.

It wiggled

and wiggled
and wiggled.

But later, at recess,
Kara won the sack race!
She was so excited
she forgot her wiggly tooth.

She didn't think about it
during lunch.

Or when she went
back to class.

"You were great in the sack race,"
Jim said to Kara.

Kara smiled at Jim.

"Your tooth!" yelled Jim.
Everyone stared at Kara.

"It's gone!" said Tanya.

"It is?" said Kara.
"Oh! I really lost my tooth!
But I don't know where!"

"We'll help you find it,"
said all the kids.

They looked everywhere—
on the playground,

in the lunchroom,

in the rest room,

in the classroom.

No tooth.

That night Kara put a note
under her pillow.
It read:

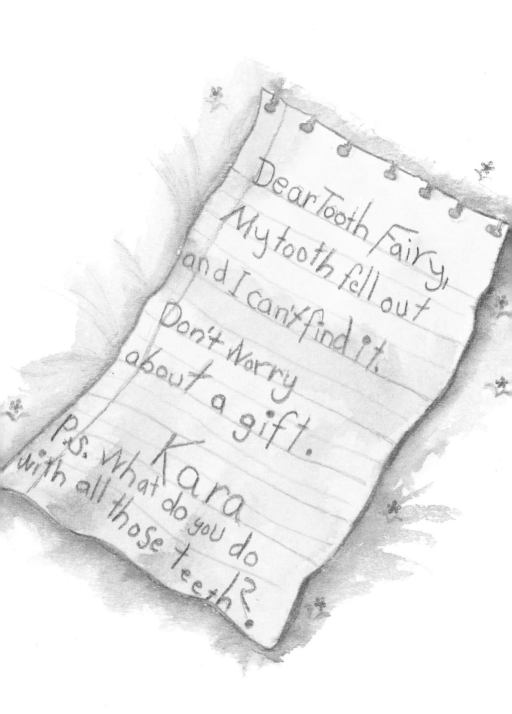

Dear Tooth Fairy,

My tooth fell out and I can't find it.

Don't worry about a gift.

Kara

P.S. What do you do with all those teeth!?

The next morning Kara found
a game and a note
under her pillow.

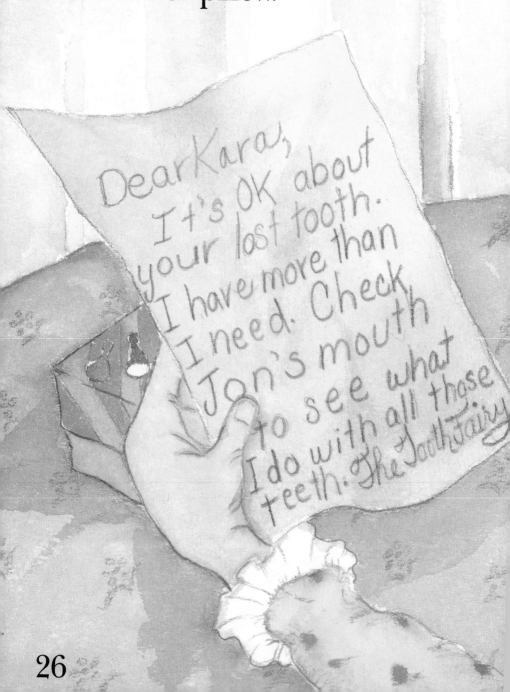

Dear Kara,
It's OK about
your lost tooth.
I have more than
I need. Check
Jon's mouth
to see what
I do with all those
teeth. The Tooth Fairy

Kara ran downstairs.
"Smile for me, Jon," she said.

Jon smiled.
He had a tiny white tooth.

Kara laughed and said,
"Now I know what the Tooth Fairy
does with all those teeth."

As she smiled,
Kara felt another loose tooth
right next to her nice new gap.
She wiggled it with her finger
and showed it to Jon.

30

"Guess what, Jon?"
she said.

31

"We're going to keep that
Tooth Fairy very busy!"